KT-379-470

This book belongs to:

....

....

Written by Jillian Harker
Illustrated by Andy Everitt-Stewart

This edition published by Parragon in 2010

Parragon
Queen Street House
4 Queen Street
BATH, BA1 1HE, UK

Copyright © Parragon Books Ltd 2006
All rights reserved. No part of this publication may be reproduced,
stored in a retrieval system, or transmitted in any form or by any
means, electronic, mechanical, photocopying, recording, or otherwise,
without the prior consent of the copyright owner.

ISBN 978-1-4054-7155-8
Printed in China

Come and Play, Oakey

Bath New York Singapore Hong Kong Cologne Delhi Melbourne

Oakey and Dad were walking
through the woods.

"Hello!" said a voice. "Would you like to play?"
Squirrel scampered out from behind a tree.
"All right," smiled Oakey.

"Let's climb some trees," suggested Squirrel, but Oakey wasn't sure.

"What if I fall?" he asked. "I haven't tried this before."

"There's no need to worry that
you might fall," Squirrel told him.
"It really isn't that hard at all.
I'll show you how to do it."

And he did.

Dad nodded to Oakey.
"You can try. Go ahead."

"You'll find out how much fun it is—
I'm sure of that!" Squirrel said.
So Oakey gave it a try.
"This really is fun!" he laughed.

"What's all the noise?" said
a voice. Dormouse poked her head
through the leaves.

"Why have you woken me up?" she
asked. "Have you come to play with me?"

"Um...all right," mumbled Oakey.

"Good! Let's swing from this
branch," suggested Dormouse.
   But Oakey wasn't sure.
"What if I get it wrong?"
he asked. "I haven't tried
this before."

"There's no need to worry about getting it wrong," Dormouse smiled. "You won't be wrong for long. I'll show you how to do it."

And she did.

Dad nodded to Oakey.
"You can try. Go ahead."
"I'm sure that you'll
enjoy it!" Dormouse said.

So Oakey gave it a try.
"I *am* enjoying it!" he laughed.

"Well then, come and play with me," said a voice.
"And you'll really have a good time."
  Oakey looked down. Otter was watching from under
the tree.

"Follow me!" he called.
So Oakey and his friends ran after Otter.

"Let's swim," said Otter.
But Oakey wasn't sure.
"What if the water gets in my eyes?" he asked. "I've never tried it before."

"If the water gets in your eyes, it won't really be a surprise. It happens to everyone," explained Otter. "Anyway, I'll show you how to do it."

And he did.

Dad nodded to Oakey.
"You can try. Go ahead."

"You'll have a great time, I promise!"
Otter said.

"Now it's time for my game," Oakey told his friends.
"Let's play leapfrog."

"Oh dear!" said Squirrel. "I've never tried this."
"Neither have I," added Dormouse. "I'm not sure."
"Me neither," agreed Otter.
"We don't know if we should," they all said at once.
"What if we're not very good?"

"You should always try," Oakey encouraged them, "and I'll tell you why. You showed me that trying something new is fun. And besides, good friends will show you how it's done!"

Would they give it a try?
With Oakey's help, they thought they would.
And what did Oakey say?

"I knew you could!" cried Oakey.
"You just needed someone to show you how."